The Principal's on the Roof

A Fletcher Mystery

The Principal's on the Roof

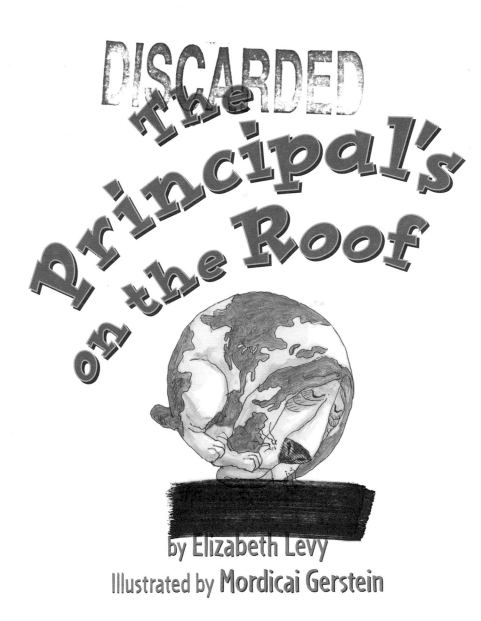

by Elizabeth Levy

Illustrated by Mordicai Gerstein

Aladdin

New York London Toronto Sydney Singapore

To Alice and Ella—E. L.

This book is a work of fiction. Any references to historical events, real people, or real locales are used fictitiously. Other names, characters, places, and incidents are the product of the author's imagination, and any resemblance to actual events or locales or persons, living or dead, is entirely coincidental.

First Aladdin Paperbacks edition October 2002
Text copyright © 2002 by Elizabeth Levy
Illustrations copyright © 2002 by Mordicai Gerstein

ALADDIN PAPERBACKS
An imprint of Simon & Schuster Children's Publishing Division
1230 Avenue of the Americas, New York, NY 10020

Also available in an Aladdin paperback edition.
Designed by Lisa Vega
The text of this book was set in ACaslon Regular.

Printed in the United States of America
10 9 8 7 6 5 4 3 2 1

Library of Congress Control Number 2002106063
ISBN 0-689-84630-4

Contents

One

There's No Accounting for Taste

"Jill, honey, come quick!" shouted Jill's mother. "Our neighbors are bringing home the baby."

I flicked my long ears. Jill had been sitting on the porch reading a book to me. She loves to do that, and I love to listen to the sound of her voice. Lately we had been reading more books than ever. Jill's school was having a reading marathon. The marathon was called "Read the Ladder to Success." Each week the principal, Mr. Leonard, would mark down how many books the kids read. Every hundred books meant a rung on the ladder. When they

got to a thousand books, the principal promised to

94 9 Books climb a real ladder and spend the morning on the roof with a microphone reading to the kids.

Now, if you asked me, roofs are for cats and pigeons, not principals. But nobody asked me. And I could feel the excitement building. By Friday, the last day of April, the kids had read 949 books.

I love books. When Jill's reading, she's usually sitting in one place. Ten-year-olds never sit still very long. I'm a basset hound who can sit in one place for a very long time.

Jill jumped up, pushing me off her lap. "The baby!" she shrieked.

"Why do humans get so excited about seeing a baby of their own kind?"

asked Jasper, the flea who lives on me. When Jasper came out of his cocoon there was nobody around to ooh and ahh. Flea eggs turn into cocoons and then into fleas. Jasper was on his own until he found a warm dog—me. Jasper and I have a beautiful friendship. He keeps the other fleas off me. He was my only friend before I found my humans.

I followed Jill and her mother down the front path. The Pryors, our next-door neighbors, were getting out of the car with the new baby, who smelled quite peculiar, wrapped in a pink blanket. She smelled sweet and sour, kind of like one of those good Chinese dishes that Jill and her mother are always ordering.

"Ohhhhh! She's so cute," cooed Jill's mother. "What's her name?"

"Well," said Mr. Pryor. "If we didn't have a cat named Alice, that might have been the name we

gave her. Instead, we're calling her Ella."

"Ella's a wonderful name," said Jill. "I can baby-sit for her sometime. I can read her stories."

"I'm sure she'll love that," said Mrs. Pryor, who looked a little tired.

"Are you coming back to school soon?" Jill asked. Mrs. Pryor was the principal's secretary at Jill's school.

"Not for a few months, at least," said Mrs. Pryor. "Mr. Leonard's been terrific. He told me to take all the time I need."

"You don't want to miss seeing him go on the roof," said Jill.

"You're right. I'll try to go for the celebration," said Mrs. Pryor. "And I'll tell you a secret. He's afraid of heights."

Jill giggled.

"We'll let you go inside and rest," said Jill's mother to the Pryors. "Ella is beautiful. It's so wonderful to have a new baby in the neighborhood."

"I just hope Alice agrees with you," said Mr. Pryor. "I'm a little worried about Alice with the new baby."

"Oh, sweetie, you worry too much," said Mrs. Pryor to her husband. "He's even worried that the baby will get fleas from Alice. But our pediatrician told him not to worry."

"What is it with humans and fleas and babies?" protested Jasper. "It's a little-known fact that there are about sixteen hundred different kinds of fleas. People are always worried about getting fleas from animals, but cat fleas only like cats, not babies, just like I only like you."

"I think that's too much for people to grasp," I told Jasper.

Just then Jill's best friend, Gwen, came careening down the sidewalk with a big knapsack on her back.

"Gwen, come quick!" yelled Jill. "It's the new

baby!" Gwen ran up the sidewalk, her backpack bouncing on her back. She peered at the baby.

"Oh, Mrs. Pryor," squeaked Gwen. "She's sooo cute!"

"Oh, no," hissed Jasper into my ear. "Not Gwen, too." Gwen is Jasper's favorite human. Gwen doesn't know he exists. Humans see dogs. They even love us. But they don't usually see fleas unless they've got an itch. They don't even know that fleas have feelings. And fleas have attractions—not just to fur. Jasper likes Gwen. He thinks she's neat. Maybe it's because Jasper and Gwen have a little bit of the same personality. When Gwen's really excited she taps her braces, and when Jasper's really excited he tends to rub his antennae together.

JASPER

GWEN

"Human babies!" sniffed Jasper. "How could Gwen prefer one of them to me? I love her!"

"Well, if she could see you, she might love you too," I said.

"Hmmm," said Jasper. "I'll have to work on that."

Uh-oh, I thought to myself. I knew we had trouble ahead. I just didn't know how much.

Two

Long Time No Flea

Gwen was over at Jill's house for a sleepover. Why do they call them sleepovers? When ten-year-olds get together, they do everything except sleep. Luckily for me, one of the things they like to do is eat a lot. I get to scarf up all the crumbs. To my great delight, Jill took out a little salami for a snack. Salami makes my heart flutter. Gwen knows this, and she snuck me a slice. I can understand why Jasper has such a soft spot for the girl.

Jill's mother made macaroni and cheese for dinner, and Jill snuck me a little under the table. After

dinner Jill and Gwen made popcorn and watched a video. I got to eat everything they dropped. Then Jill's mom made cookies, and we all ate cookies and milk. Finally even I was full.

Around nine o'clock we went up to Jill's bedroom on the second floor. Gwen carried her knapsack. Her knapsack was so full that she looked bent over, almost like a witch in a fairy tale, as she climbed the stairs.

When we got to Jill's bedroom, Gwen plunked her knapsack on the guest bed and opened it. I sniffed around to see if there were any snacks in there. She had brought her toothbrush and nightgown, and that was about it—except for books. She pulled a whole bunch of mysteries from her knapsack.

It's a myth that animals only like books about animals. I like a good human mystery as much as anybody. Humans are always surprised when they come home and they can't find the book they were

reading. We animals read while humans are out, and we don't always put the books back where they left them.

Jasper loves joke books. This is his favorite joke.

"Knock-knock."

"Who's there?"

"Flea."

"Flea who?"

"Flea's a jolly good fellow!" cackles Jasper every time he tells me that joke, which is often. The sound of a cackling flea is not a pretty sound.

"Do you think you brought enough books?" Jill asked Gwen.

"I'm doing research," said Gwen. "I'm writing my own mystery. It's called 'The Mystery on the Roof,' by J. Fletcher."

Jill scratched me behind my ear, which I love.

"Is it a shaggy-dog story? Is that why you called yourself Fletcher?" she teased.

"Dogs can't write," said Gwen. "I decided to use a pen name. It makes it sound more like a real book."

"J. Fletcher?!" chortled Jasper into my ear. "Did you hear that? She named herself after you and me. I must be the J."

"She doesn't know you exist," I reminded him. "You're a flea. She can't even see you."

"What's the J for?" Jill asked. "Me?"

Gwen shrugged. "Maybe. I just had an urge to use the letter J. It looks distinguished."

Jasper held himself to his full one-eighth of an inch. "I'm distinguished," he said. His little antennae were twitching so much that I couldn't help but scratch myself.

"Ouch!" said Jasper. "Shh . . . maybe Gwen will

read us her story. I wonder if it has a flea in it. Every good mystery needs a flea."

"Every good mystery needs a flea bath," I muttered.

Jill's mother came in to say good night. Jill's mom was in the Parent-Teacher Organization that was sponsoring the reading marathon. "What are you girls reading tonight?" asked Jill's mother.

"Gwen wrote a story," said Jill. "Can we read that and have it count as one of our books?"

"I don't see why not," said Jill's mother.

Jasper got very excited when he saw Gwen pull out some manuscript pages with lots of black lines through them.

"Do you want me to read it?" asked Jill's mother. "I came up to read you a story."

"I'd better do it," said Gwen. "It's just a sloppy copy."

"I've got to get a closer seat," said Jasper. Fleas don't fly, but that flea flipped fabulously to Gwen's fifth finger. From there he flipped himself up near

JASPER FLIPPING FABULOUSLY

Gwen's shoulder. I was worried that she would flick the flea off, but she smiled.

"My story is called 'The Mystery on the Roof,'" said Gwen.

Creatures from outer space move on silent cats' paws. They live on our roofs and they try to control our lives.

"How do they do that?" asked Jill.

"Uh, I'm not sure," said Gwen. "I haven't got every detail worked out. Let me go on.

These creatures cannot be seen by human

eyes. They are not human, but they make humans sneeze.

"Aliens who make humans sneeze . . . how do they do that?" Jill interrupted.

"I haven't figured that out either. Stop giving me criticism before I finish," said Gwen.

"Well, I think you should know. It's important."

Gwen tapped her braces. She always did that while she was thinking.

I saw Jasper jump close to her ear.

Gwen giggled.

"I've got it. My aliens will have antennae that they can tickle people with. That will make them sneeze."

"Isn't she brilliant?" sighed Jasper.

Gwen paused. She didn't know that putting in antennae had made a flea's day.

"Go on," said Jill.

"Uh . . . I don't have much more," admitted Gwen. "I'll have to figure out what the aliens do once they make people sneeze."

"Yeah, it needs a really good ending," said Jill.

"Now that I've got that sneezing problem solved, it'll be great. I'm going to take it into school and show it to Mrs. Neville. I want the whole class to count it as one of their books."

"I don't know," said Jill. "It needs work."

Gwen frowned. It's never easy to criticize a writer.

Jasper was jumping up and down on Gwen's shoulder. "It's absolutely fabulous!" he squeaked into her ear. Gwen scratched her earlobe, but of course she couldn't hear him.

"Get down from there!" I growled to him. He was making me nervous.

Jill started to laugh. "Uh-oh, now Fletcher's

weighing in. I'm not sure Fletcher likes your story," she said to Gwen. "Or maybe he doesn't want his name on it."

I didn't want Gwen to think that. I was flattered that she had used my name. I wagged my tail back and forth, back and forth.

"See, he does like it," said Gwen. She knelt down and took my chin in her hands. "Thanks, Fletcher," she said. "Your opinion means a lot to me."

It meant a lot to *me* that Jasper took that opportunity to flip from her finger to my nose. I wrinkled my nose. Gwen frowned. She thought I was commenting on her writing.

Gwen stood up and faced Jill. "What do you think I should do to make my story better?" she asked seriously.

"Miss Neville is always telling us to write what you know," said Jill. "I don't think you know too much about aliens on the roof."

Gwen tapped her braces. She always does that when she's excited.

"Let's go out on the roof now," she said. She looked at Jill's mom. "Can we do that? Maybe I'll get inspiration."

"Well, it is a beautiful night," said Jill's mother.

There was a balcony off of Jill's bedroom. Jill's mother opened the door.

"Come on, Fletcher," said Jill.

Now, I love the girl, but sometimes I think she has no appreciation for how comfy it can be just staying in one place. I followed her out. I knew she'd be disappointed if I didn't.

I have to admit, they were right. It was a beautiful late-April night. The moon was nearly full. Once we were outside, I was glad that I had come. I put my head on Jill's leg. A human leg smells

warm and toasty. Jill's hand snuggled against my ear, and she scratched. I heard Jasper giggle as he jumped to get out of her way.

"There's the school," said Jill, pointing to the flat roof very close by. I had never noticed the school roof before. It looked dark and big at night.

"A perfect landing place for an alien spaceship," said Gwen, scribbling onto her manuscript.

"Maybe there could be an alien principal who falls off the roof," suggested Jill. "That would make a funny mystery."

"Maybe," said Gwen, tapping her braces. She took out her pen and wrote again on her paper.

Just then the phone rang. Jill's mother got up. "Are you girls okay out here alone?" she asked.

"Sure," said Jill. "I don't think we have to worry about any real aliens landing on our roof."

Jill's mother laughed. "Well, just stay away from

the railing. I'll get the phone." She went inside.

There was a rustling through the trees. My ears twitched back and forth.

"What's that?" asked Jill.

"Is it a bat?!" exclaimed Gwen. Humans are afraid of bats.

I saw a pair of yellow eyes peering through the leaves. The hairs on the back of my neck stood up.

"My mysterious alien with yellow eyes," whispered Gwen.

"Uh . . . what if it's a real bat?" asked Jill in a scared voice. "I find bats scarier than aliens."

"Me too," whispered Jasper.

A BAT-FLEA

"Why?" I asked him.

"If you're a flea on a bat," said Jasper, "you have to live in a cave and hang upside down all day." He shuddered and burrowed his way into my fur. "Let's get out of here," he said.

I looked out at the moon. I heard a high-pitched complaining sound in the trees. I wasn't sure it was a bat, but whoever or whatever it was, I knew it was unhappy. I had lived on the streets. I knew what it was like to feel all alone. I wondered why the creature with yellow eyes was so unhappy.

Three

What's Black and White and Has the Blues?

When I first came to live with Jill, Jill's mother insisted I go about on a leash all the time. Now that they know I am not the kind of dog who wanders off, they allow me to go out on my own.

On Monday, it was a beautiful day. Jasper and I decided to go pick Jill up at school. There's a hole in the bushes between Jill's house and the Pryors' that makes a shortcut to the school. I never like to take any more steps than I have to.

I heard a hissing sound. I looked up. There in the tree was a black-and-white cat with a big, big

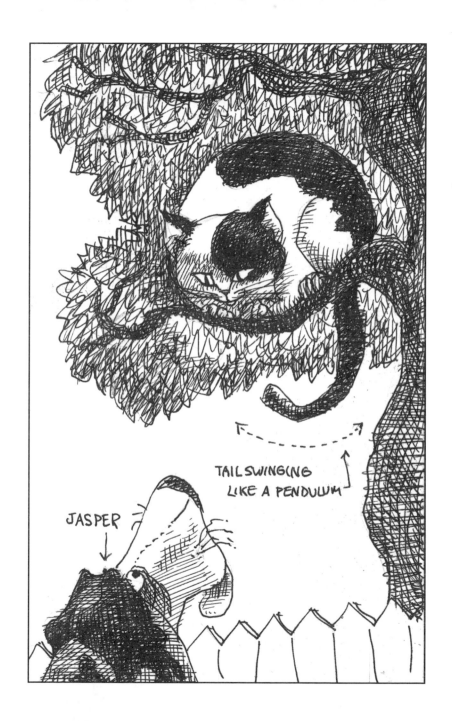

belly. Her tail was twitching back and forth, back and forth like a pendulum. I recognized her. I often saw her sitting in the window at the Pryors' house, but I had never seen her outside before, even on the most lovely of spring days.

"Some pets have all the luck!" she wailed in a sing-song voice, out of tune.

"Excuse me?" I asked.

"Some dogs have all the luck!" she caterwauled.

"Who are you?"

"I am the cat of despair," she said.

"I'm Fletcher," I said. "We've never properly met even though we're neighbors."

"Fletch me a pail of my tears . . . because I've got buckets of them." wailed the cat.

"Excuse me," I said.

"Once I lived the life of a millionaire.

eating my cat food. I didn't have a care. . . ."

"You've got a lousy voice." I had to tell her the truth.

"I've got the blues." She sighed and stretched.

"The blues?"

"Yes, haven't you heard of the blues? It's when you feel blue all over. Nothing can make you feel better except singing out the sadness. They say it's raining cats and dogs on stormy Monday. but Tuesday's just as bad." She hit a particularly off-pitch note.

RAINING CATS + DOGS

"How do you get a cat to stop singing the blues?" I asked.

"Have her stuffed," suggested Jasper.

"Is that a flea?" asked the cat.

"I'm Jasper," said Jasper. "Please stop singing."

"A flea can flee—but I can't flee from these low-down blues. . . ." she sang.

Jasper put his antennae over his ears. I put my paws over mine.

Finally the cat paused. "Is something wrong?" she asked.

"Your voice," I said, honestly. "What are you doing out of the house? I've only seen you through the window before."

"I'm a house cat. My name is Alice. From the day the Pryors brought me home, I lived inside, but then . . ." Alice paused and began singing again. "My baby came home—and I'm out in the cold. . . ."

"It's not cold," I told her. "It's a lovely day."

"Look, Fletcher," said Jasper. "Maybe you like listening to her sad story, but I think we should go to school and pick up Gwen and Jill."

"Gwen doesn't even know you exist," I explained

to Jasper. "And you can't just leave a cat with the blues. It's bad luck."

"I think that's supposed to be a black cat," said Alice. "I'm black and white, and blue all over."

"And a little melodramatic, may I add," I said.

Alice sighed again. She stretched. Then she carefully climbed down the tree trunk headfirst, something I couldn't do in a million years. She came to our level.

"Who's the flea in your ear?" she asked. Alice had good hearing. We dogs think we can hear things a mile away, but nothing was wrong with this cat's ears.

"Jasper," I said. "He's your neighbor too."

"What's he in a twitch about?" asked Alice.

"We like to be in front of the school when it lets out," I said. "Jill and her best friend, Gwen, look for us."

"Kids," muttered Alice. "I hate them."

"What kind of creature hates kids?" asked Jasper.

Jasper had a point. It does seem that most people and animals like kids. It's one of those things that makes the world a better place.

"What do you have against kids?" I asked Alice.

"It's not all kids," said Alice. "It's the one they just brought into my house. I was living very happily with two adults. There was always somebody to feed me and to rub up against. I was the apple of their eye. Then slowly Mrs. Pryor began to look a little like an apple herself."

"She was pregnant," I said.

"Now you tell me. I thought she was just opening too many cans of tuna. Then they brought home a baby! Ella," muttered Alice. "They might as well have called it Ella the Great. They spend all their time looking at her. Nobody even noticed when I went outside."

"Cheer up," I said. "Little Ella will grow up into a girl just like Jill or her friend Gwen. She'll pet you and make you feel good."

"All she does is sleep and poop," moaned Alice. "She doesn't even use a litter box."

"Stop moping around," I said. " If you want you can come with us to the school."

"No thanks," said Alice. "I don't like to travel much. . . ." She paused. "At least on the ground." She scampered back up into the tree.

"Was that you prowling around our roof last night?" I asked her.

Alice nodded. "I'm climbing the trees of woe because you no longer love me. You don't want me in your lap. I'm a sap for a nap. . . ."

"A blues song about a nap," I said to Jasper. "I like that cat's style."

"Not me," said Jasper. "She's making my antennae ache."

I told Miss Alice that we had to go. She didn't seem to pay any attention. When a cat is stuck in the blues, there's no reaching her.

Four

Sour Puss

When we got to school, classes had already been dismissed. There was a huge crowd outside the front door. Yet nobody seemed to be getting on the buses or walking home.

"Fire drill," said Jasper. We had learned that sometimes all the kids go outside for what they call a fire drill.

"I don't think so," I said to Jasper. "Everyone is milling about. In a fire drill the kids are all in straight lines." I sniffed around. I can find Jill's smell through a zillion different scents. I made my way to her side.

"Hi, Fletcher," Jill said, bending down and giving me a hug. It certainly didn't seem like a fire drill. I wagged my tail at her. She was standing in the middle of a bunch of kids, but none of them was Gwen.

"Find out where Gwen is?" asked Jasper in a worried voice. Jill and Gwen were rarely apart.

Sometimes Jasper forgets that Jill and I don't really speak the same language. I can understand what humans say, but I just can't come out and ask humans things in words—not the way Jasper and I and other animals can talk to each other.

"Hey, Jill!" I heard a mocking voice say. "Where's Gwen? Is she going to follow the principal up on the roof? Is she up there asking aliens for a better ending for her story?"

Jill put her hands on her hips, something she almost always does when she's angry.

"Look, Chris," she said. "It was great that Gwen read her story in front of the class. You shouldn't have made fun of her. And you didn't need to make that big fake sneeze. She is proud of that story. And she didn't have to read it to everybody. She wanted to."

"I bet Gwen's slinking around because she was embarrassed that her story was so lame," said Chris. "Aliens with long antennae . . . give me a break."

"Oh my goodness!" gasped Jasper. "She read her story out loud and that twit didn't like it. Let me at him. I'll make that critic itch."

"Will you calm down?" I growled.

"Why is your dog growling?" asked Chris. "I thought he was a gentle dog."

"Fletcher's very gentle," said Jill. "That wasn't a growl. Sometimes he just feels like making silly sounds, don't you, boy?"

Humans love to think that we're silly. I rolled over on my back and let Jill scratch my belly. When in doubt, let humans scratch your belly.

Jasper was still upset. He jumped onto my stomach to avoid being crushed. "Get up," he urged. "We've got to look for Gwen."

Just then there was a loud voice that came from the roof. "Testing, testing!"

"It's Mr. Leonard," said Jill, sounding excited. "He's testing to see if the bullhorn works and we can hear him from the roof. Where is Gwen? I know she wants to see this."

"I told you," said Chris. "She's probably looking for aliens on the roof."

Just then Gwen came around the corner. Her hair was a little messy. And she looked as if she had been somewhere dirty.

"Where were you?" asked Jill.

Gwen tapped her braces nervously. "Well, I just wanted to see what was really on the school roof. When Mr. Leonard went up, I tried to follow him, but one of the teachers saw me and made me get down. I slipped on the last rung and fell."

"Maybe you should use that in your story," teased Chris. "The writer who fell to earth."

"Gwen will come up with the perfect ending on her own," said Jill. I liked the girl's loyalty. We dogs appreciate loyalty.

"I was doing research for my story," said Gwen. "I wanted to get the details right. Chris is right. It isn't quite there yet."

"Don't let Chris bother you," Jill said. "The rest of the class loved it. And remember, Mrs. Neville thought it was great."

"Yeah," said Gwen. "But Chris said it was lame."

I licked Gwen's hand. She was so human. She

forgot about the good reviews and just remembered the bad ones.

Mr. Leonard came down the ladder. "I think I'll be fine," he announced. "The weather report looks good, and it's a nice view from up there," he said.

"Have you chosen the story you're going to read?" Mrs. Neville asked Mr. Leonard.

"I thought I'd read *The Cat in the Hat*," said Mr. Leonard.

"I have a suggestion," said Mrs. Neville. "Gwen is writing a very funny story that takes place on a roof. She read it to our class. It's called 'The Mystery on the Roof.'"

"Why, that's a great idea!" said Mr. Leonard, stroking his chin. "Using an original story for the ladder of success. Gwen, give me a copy, I'll make it the 1001st story. Just like the 1001 stories of the Arabian nights."

"I'll go home and make it even better," said Gwen excitedly. "You'll see, Mr. Leonard. I'll make it into one of the best stories ever."

"Just give Mr. Leonard a clean copy tomorrow morning," said Mrs. Neville.

Gwen was so excited she couldn't talk about anything else except her story as we walked home. We passed the Pryors' house. I heard a sound. It was Alice walking through the grass. Her tail was twitching, not a good sign in a cat.

Alice was wailing. "The baby's inside—and I'm on the outs. . ." I couldn't believe that she hadn't run out of blues songs.

"What's that noise?" asked Jill. She looked down through the bushes.

Alice jumped easily up on a garbage can and then up to the garage roof. "It was an alien, I'm sure," said Gwen.

I hoped she was kidding. A human who couldn't tell a cat from an alien was hopeless.

"An alien on silent cat's paws wailed into the night," Gwen shouted as she wrote in her notebook. "The alien wanted people to sneeze because it reminded him of home. On his planet a sneeze meant 'I love you.' Let's go to your house. I'll write the ending and read it to you. This is so great!"

"I got the blues and she's happy," moaned Alice.

"She's writing a very important story," said Jasper.

"What's so important about her story?" Alice asked.

"It's going to be read on the roof tomorrow," I explained. "Everybody will be there. I heard the Pryors say that they wanted to come."

"Come on, Fletcher," said Jill. "We've got to help Gwen finish her story. It's got to be perfect."

"We've got to go," I said to Alice.

"Oh sure, leave me all alone . . . again."

"I just hope Gwen writes a happy ending," said Jasper. "I like happy endings."

"Happy endings aren't real," said Alice.

"You know what you are?" said Jasper. "A sour puss."

Alice looked a little hurt.

"Don't mind him," I said to Alice. "I kind of like your blues. They show that life's hard on the outside, but good on the inside—kind of like salami."

Five

Giant Sneezes on the Roof

The next morning Jill's mother got dressed in an "I ♥ TO READ" T-shirt.

"I'm going to walk you to school today," she announced at breakfast. "I called into work and told them that I'd be a few hours late. I want to see the moment that Mr. Leonard goes up on the roof and reads Gwen's story."

Jasper jumped up and down. "Get them to take us!!" he screamed in my ear.

"Calm down," I said. "We're animals. We're only invited to school on special days."

"This *is* a special day. Come on, give them that look!"

"All right," I sighed. I took a deep breath. There *is* a look that we canines can give humans that they find irresistible. But all dogs have been warned not to use it too much.

I padded up to Jill's mother just as she was getting Jill's jacket. I sat down right in front of her. I cocked my head to the side. That's the look that really gets them. You cock your head to the side and open your mouth just a little. Then you look up at them with your brown eyes.

Jill's mother looked at me. She bent down and scratched me behind the ear. I wagged my tail, hoping she'd understand that we wanted to go with her. Sometimes adults don't get dog language as well as kids do.

Luckily at that moment, Gwen came to the door.

She was dressed in a black-and-white T-shirt. "Thanks, Jill, for your help yesterday. I put in all the changes. I printed it out on the computer, and I'm going to give it to Mr. Leonard," she said. "It's really, really good now."

"We've got to get going," said Jill's mother. They started to go out the door. I stood in front of them and gave them "the look" again.

"What's the matter, boy?" Jill asked.

"He wants to come watch Mr. Leonard read my story," said Gwen. "I know that's what he wants. He wants to come see the principal on the roof."

"I could hug that girl," whispered Jasper.

"Luckily, your antennae aren't long enough," I told him.

As we walked outside, we ran into the Pryors. Mr. Pryor had the baby wrapped around his chest.

"Oh, she's in the snuggly!" cooed Gwen.

"Yes," said Mrs. Pryor. "This is Ella's first outing. I promised Mr. Leonard that I'd take her to see him on the roof."

When we got to school, I realized that the principal going up on the roof was a very big deal. A lot of the reporters from the local newspapers and the local TV station were gathered on the front lawn of the school. Even the fire department was there.

Mr. Leonard spotted Mr. and Mrs. Pryor and came running up to them. "You brought the baby!" he cried in that voice that humans use only on babies and puppies.

"This is Ella," said Mrs. Pryor. "When she grows up I'll tell her when she was just a couple of weeks old she saw her mom's boss go up on the school roof."

"As long as I don't fall down," teased Mr. Leonard. "Gwen, do you have your story for me?"

"Yes," said Gwen. "I printed out a clean copy."

Just then Sasha Hughes, the star of a local TV show, "Sasha Says," came up to us. "Mr. Leonard," she said, grabbing his arm. "I understand that the children have read one thousand books for today's event."

"Yes, they did," said Mr. Leonard. "And the 1001st is going to be a story written by one of our very own students."

"That's me!" squeaked Gwen.

Jill giggled. But Gwen stepped up to the microphone like a pro. "I haven't just been reading! I've been writing, too! Our class read my story, 'The Mystery on the Roof.' I used a pen name, J. Fletcher, because it sounded more mysterious, but I don't mind everyone knowing that it's me."

"How cute!" said Sasha Hughes. "Folks, we have a budding writer."

"Oh, I'm not just budding," said Gwen. "There's

a twist at the end that's going to surprise everyone and—"

"Thank you very much," said Sasha Hughes. She wrestled the microphone away from Gwen. "But now I think we'll cut to the real story of this day. The fact that the principal of our neighborhood's school cares so much about kids reading that he is willing to go up on the roof."

Mr. Leonard started to climb up the ladder on the side of the building. When he got up to the top of the roof, he waved down to everybody. The custodian attached a bullhorn to a pulley and sent it up to him.

Mr. Leonard took the bullhorn. Suddenly he gave a big sneeze. He almost toppled over. Then he sneezed again! The sneezes echoed across the schoolyard.

"Hey!" shouted Chris. He pointed a finger at

Gwen. "Her silly story about antennae and sneezes is coming true."

"Excuse me," said Sasha Hughes. "What is that about sneezes and the story?"

"Gwen's story," said Chris. "It's all about an invisible alien with antennae that tickle. Personally, I thought it wasn't very believable, but now the principal's sneezing . . . so . . ."

"You mean the author knew the principal would sneeze? . . ."

"Well," admitted Chris, "I guess she couldn't know. . . ."

"Unless," said Sasha Hughes, "unless . . . perhaps she put sneezing powder in her pages."

"You know," said Chris, "that's exactly the kind of thing Gwen would try. Yesterday she tried to go up on the roof."

AHCHOO! ACHOO! ACHOO! ACHOO! ACHOO!

SNEEZING POWDER

"Ah ha!" said Sasha Hughes. "So we have a publicity-mad writer who would do anything to get her story read by the principal. Is that what you're saying?"

"Uh . . ." stammered Chris, "I think it's what *you're* saying."

Gwen looked at Jill desperately. "I didn't do anything, honestly."

"I believe you," whispered Jill. "But I'm not sure anybody else does!"

"Ladies and gentlemen!" said Sasha Hughes. "We've got a breaking story and a little bit of a scandal. It seems that even among the pint-sized writers, there are some who would do anything for publicity!"

Gwen's face turned bright red. "I didn't do anything! Chris was just jealous my story got picked."

There was another loud sneeze from the roof.

Even Mrs. Neville was looking at Gwen suspiciously.

Gwen looked down at me as if she thought I could do something. Humans have a look just the way dogs do. It's irresistible. I didn't know what I could do. But I was going to have to do something to help.

There was another sneeze. Then my fine-tuned ears picked up a wailing sing-song sound that I had heard before. And it was coming from the roof. I wasn't sure that humans could pick up the sound, but I was pretty sure that it wasn't sneezing powder up on the roof. I knew who it was. But now I had to get the humans to go up there and prove that I was right.

Six

Tabby or Not Tabby— That Is the Question

"Roof! Roof!" I barked.

Jill patted my head absentmindedly. "Shh, Fletcher," she said. "We've got a real problem on our hands."

"Roof! Roof!" I repeated. Oh, why couldn't those humans understand? I needed Jill and Gwen to go up on the roof. I knew the answer was up there. But they ignored me. They thought I was making dog sounds: "Ruff! Ruff!"

I knew that Alice was up there somewhere, causing trouble. A cat with the blues is always trouble.

"We've got to go up ourselves," hissed Jasper into my ear.

"Are you kidding!" I said. "How am I going to get up on the roof?"

"I don't expect you to fly," said Jasper. "Take the ladder!"

"Roof! Roof!" I muttered. I tried once more to get Jill's attention, but she was too preoccupied arguing with Chris and Mrs. Neville.

"Climb! Climb!" urged Jasper. I put my front paws on the bottom rung of the ladder, and I pulled myself up. Basset hounds are not meant to climb ladders. We are built for lying in the grass and hunting rabbits. We are not climbers.

"Look!" Sasha Hughes said to her cameraman. "The dog is climbing up the ladder. Get a picture of that before anyone else does."

"Great," I muttered to Jasper. "I'm not doing

this to get my picture on TV."

"Just keep climbing," said Jasper. Jasper jumped out to the edge of my nose so he could see where we were going. Meanwhile, I could hear poor Mr. Leonard sneezing and sneezing up on the roof.

I reached the last rung of the ladder. I hauled myself onto the roof.

"I thought Alice was causing the trouble," I said to Jasper when I looked around. "But she's not here." There was nothing up on the roof except poor Mr. Leonard sneezing. He was sneezing so much that he couldn't even begin to read Gwen's story.

Jasper's antennae twitched. "Look behind the air-conditioning units."

The roof had three big air-conditioning units that had just been put on during the last renovation. "Go," urged Jasper. "I thought I saw something move in the shadows."

I took a deep breath. Heights were not to my liking and the air-conditioning unit was built very close to the edge of the roof. But I walked behind the unit.

I heard a soft wailing sound. "Tabby or not tabby— that is the question."

"Alice!" I exclaimed.

"I know the Pryors are down there," she said. "I thought if they saw how desperate I am, they might . . ."

"Don't do anything stupid," I said.

But she did. She whizzed by me. She took a leap and landed on Mr. Leonard's head.

Mr. Leonard's hands flew up. He leaned forward. I rushed to him and grabbed hold of his jacket with my teeth and held on tight. Alice was perched precariously on the pinnacle of his pate.

Mr. Leonard sneezed. But I held on. Mr. Leonard

scuttled backward. He was safe. Mr. Leonard waved to everybody down on the ground. "I'm okay!" he shouted. "It was just a cat. I'm allergic to cats."

"It's Alice!" shrieked Mrs. Pryor. "What's Alice doing up there?"

"What indeed?" I asked Alice.

"I didn't know the principal was allergic!" wailed Alice. "Now I'm even making my owner's boss sneeze. She'll get rid of me for sure."

"Stop singing the blues," I said to her. "You almost got Jill's best friend in trouble. Down there, they thought Gwen had laced her paper with sneezing powder."

"I just can't do anything right!" wailed Alice.

"Will you stop feeling sorry for yourself?" I told her.

"Mr. Leonard!" yelled Sasha Hughes. "Can you tell us what is happening?"

"I'm not sure," said Mr. Leonard. "Jill's dog Fletcher pulled me back from the roof. I thought cats and dogs were enemies, but these two seem to know each other. If I didn't know better I'd swear they were talking."

"Go down there and make friends with the baby," I said to Alice. "That's all they want."

Alice gave me a sigh.

"Go on," Jasper told her. "Your humans have room in their hearts for a baby and you."

Alice did something I would never do in a zillion years. She took a flying leap off the roof.

Mrs. Pryor shrieked. "Oh no, Alice!" But cats can land, well, like a cat. Alice landed on the grass and daintily made her way over to the Pryors. Mrs. Pryor picked her up.

"Alice, we've missed you," said Mr. Pryor. "And I think baby Ella has missed you too."

From up on the roof, I could hear Alice purring. Mr. Leonard put his arm around me.

"I just want everybody to give three cheers for Fletcher."

"Nobody ever cheers for a flea!" said Jasper. "Fame is fleeting for a flea."

All the kids down below gave out three big lusty cheers. I must admit it felt good to hear all that cheering. A dog could get used to it. "Some of that's for you," I whispered to Jasper.

Then Mr. Leonard picked up Gwen's story. "Now," he said, "in honor of our reading marathon, I would like to read the 1001st story. The title of the story is very appropriate for today. It is 'The Mystery on the Roof.'"

I looked down from the roof. Jill had her arm around Gwen's shoulders proudly.

And then Mr. Leonard began to read.

The alien had a deep dark secret. He was rubbing his antennae together to sing the blues. He didn't know that it made humans sneeze. His song went like this: "All alone—an alien all alone always— alligators and antelopes are not aliens—," sang the alien.

"Oh no," said Jasper. "It does have a blues song."

"Just listen," I told him. "It's a good story."

The alien's song was very catching. Just like sneezes. Soon humans all over the world, especially children, were singing the alien's song. It became number one on the charts. And the alien didn't feel so alone anymore.

"There," I said to Jasper. "She did put in a happy ending. But it could have used a flea."

Jasper wiped a tear from his little eye. I wagged my tail so that Gwen and Jill would know that Jasper and I liked the story. Jill waved up to me. Gwen tapped her braces, and she gave a little wave. I swear that wave was for Jasper.